CAPTAIN DUCK

First published in hardback in Great Britain by HarperCollins Children's Books in 2002
First published in paperback by Collins Picture Books in 2003
This edition published in 2009

10 9 8 7 6

ISBN 978-0-00-730290-1

Collins Picture Books is an imprint of the Children's Division, part of HarperCollins Publishers Ltd.

HarperCollins Children's Books is a division of HarperCollins Publishers Ltd.

Text and illustrations copyright © Jez Alborough 2002

The author/illustrator asserts the moral right to be identified as the author/illustrator of the work.

A CIP catalogue record for this title is available from the British Library.

1 London Bridge Street, London SE1 9GF.

Visit our website at: www.harpercollins.co.uk

Printed and bound in China

For Dad with love

Jez Alborough

CAPTAIN DUCK

HarperCollins *Children's Books*

Pop, pop, coughs the spluttering truck.
'No more petrol left,' quacks Duck.

'It's good I stopped
near my friend Goat –

he uses petrol
in his boat.'

Duck rap-tap-taps at Goat's back door,
waits a while, then taps once more.

Still no answer, so instead,

he sneaks a peek inside Goat's shed.

'Hooray!' cries Duck. 'A stroke of luck –

petrol for my
thirsty truck.

I'll only take a drop or two…
Look, there's Frog! Where's he off to?'

He's off to take a trip on a boat.
'Hello!' calls Sheep. 'Hop in!' says Goat.

'There's one last thing I need to bring...
Now while I'm gone, don't pull that string.'

They check the map
and pack the snack.

Then suddenly,
they hear a quack.

'Ahoy there, sailors!'
comes a cry.

'Is this a boating
trip I spy?

If there are seas
to be explored,

make way... CAPTAIN DUCK'S ON BOARD!

Let's get going!
What's this thing?'

'No!' cries Frog.
'Don't pull that string!'

ROAR

Captain Kidd

The engine roars, Frog gives a shout.
'Oh, no!' screams Sheep. 'Frog's fallen out!'

PLOP

'Grab that rope,' says Duck. 'I'll steer.
Throw it out when we get near.

Ready… steady… get set… THROW!
Catch!' yells Duck. 'And here we go.

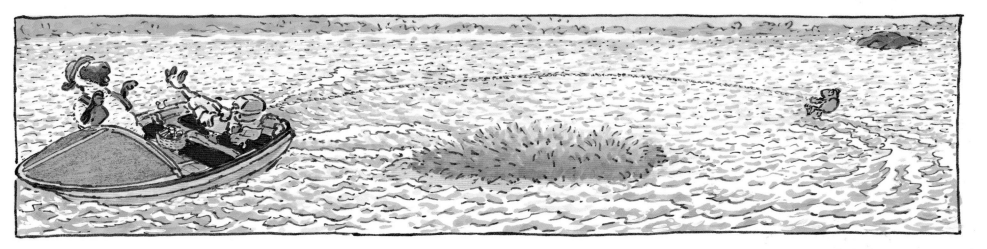

Oh please, Duck. Please don't go too far.

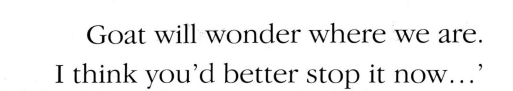

Goat will wonder where we are.
I think you'd better stop it now...'

'I can't,' yells Duck.'I don't know how.

Besides we've

only just begun…

and Frog is having so much fun.'

So Captain Duck steers the boat

far away from poor old Goat

who finds his can beside a truck.

'Aha!' he says. 'That naughty Duck.'

The little boat bobs on and on

until the river banks are gone.

Just then the engine
pop-pop-pops

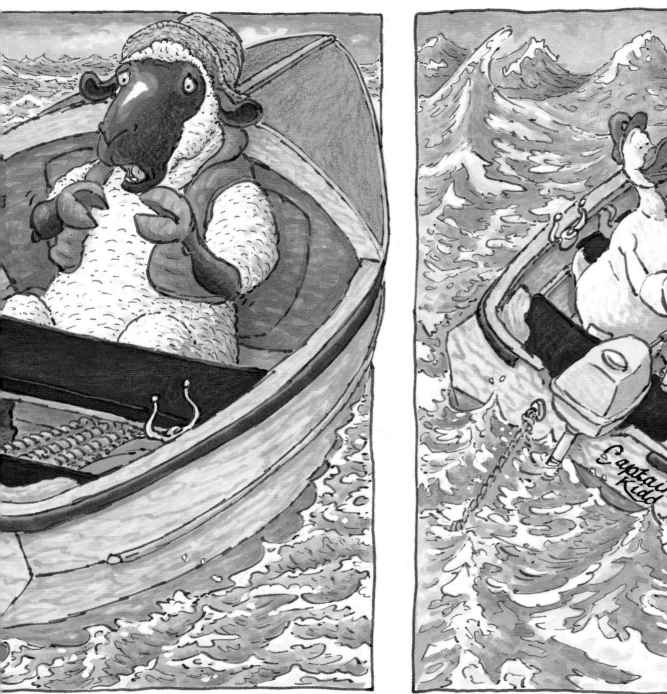

and with a final cough
it stops.

The stormy waves begin to swell.
Sheep says, 'I don't feel too well.'

'Come on,' says Duck,
'we'll row to shore.'

'We can't,'
gasps Frog.
'There's just one oar.'

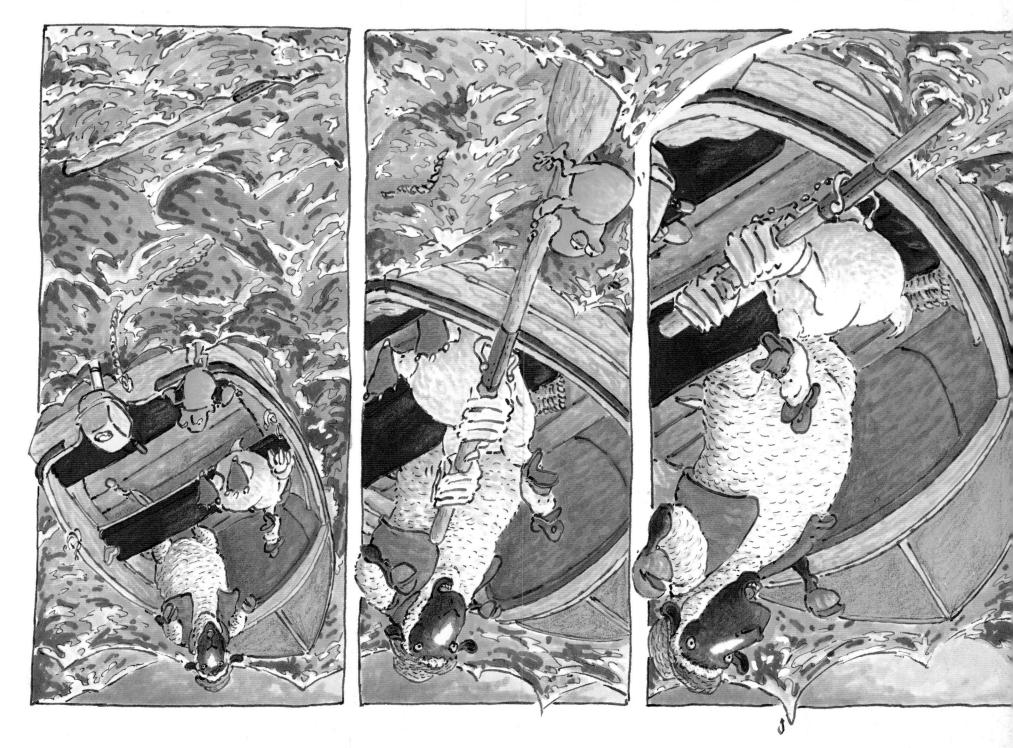

They huddle in the bobbing boat
and snuggle close to Sheep's warm coat.

And there upon the restless deep

three lost friends fall fast asleep.

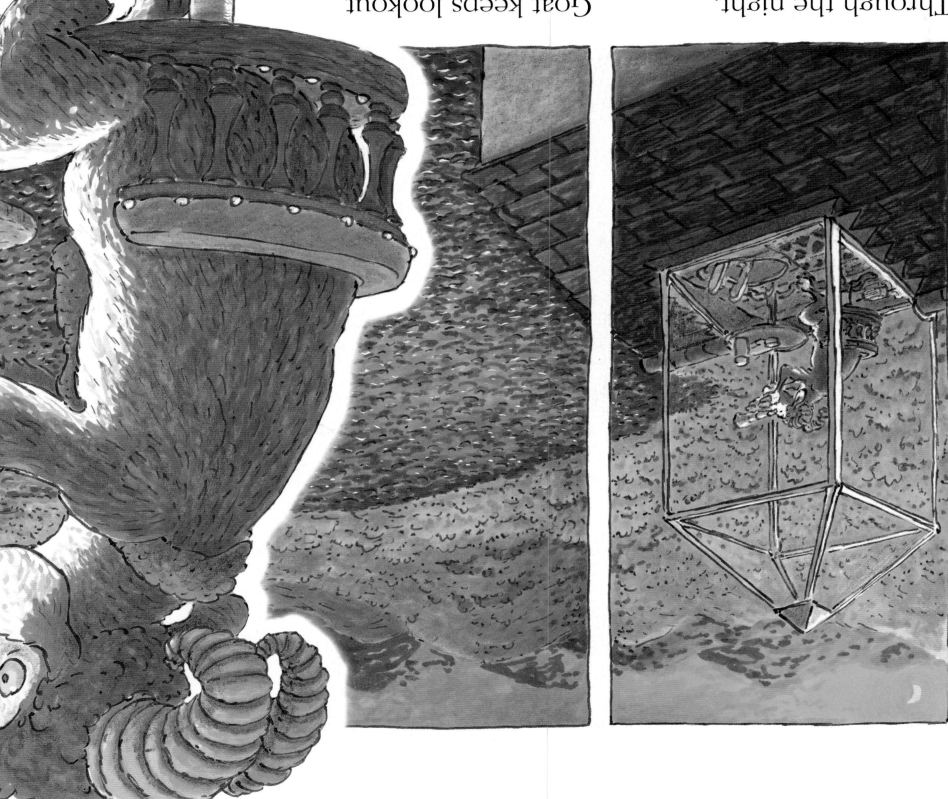

Through the night,
hour by hour.

Goat keeps lookout
from his tower.

And then at dawn,
    through bleary eyes,   upon the tide,   his boat he spies.

Sheep calls out, 'We're sorry, Goat.
We left you here...   we broke your boat!'

'Broken?' says Goat as Duck tries to hide.
'Oh, no, it just needed petrol inside.

That's why I went back for the can I keep spare.
I searched through my shed but the can wasn't there.'

'Wait!' says Frog. 'Duck was holding a can!
It was just before our boat trip began.

So Duck took the petrol.'   'That's right,' says Goat.
'Now you know why there wasn't enough in the boat.'

'ook! Duck's getting away!' Sheep cries.

'he's not!' gloats Goat   with a glint in his eyes.

'He took the petrol,
that silly Duck,

but forgot to pour it into his truck!

WATCH OUT, here comes DUCK!

HB ISBN: 978-0-00-198346-5 £10.99
PB ISBN: 978-0-00-730262-8 £5.99
PB & CD ISBN: 978-0-00-731541-3 £7.99

KATE GREENAWAY MEDAL
HIGHLY COMMENDED
PB ISBN: 978-0-00-730289-5 £6.99
PB & CD ISBN: 978-0-00-724209-2 £7.99

PB ISBN: 978-0-00-730290-1 £6.99
PB & CD ISBN: 978-0-00-721421-1 £7.99

PB ISBN: 978-0-00-730291-8 £6.99
PB & CD ISBN: 978-0-00-721219-4 £7.99

HB ISBN: 978-0-00-727326-3 £10.99
PB ISBN: 978-0-00-727327-0 £5.99

Coming soon!
PB & CD ISBN: 978-0-00-731547-5

Collect all the hilarious books in the series!

HB ISBN: 978-0-00-724355-6 £10.99
PB ISBN: 978-0-00-724356-3 £5.99

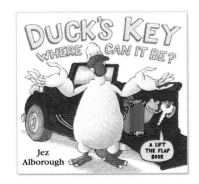

SHORTLISTED FOR THE
BOOKTRUST EARLY YEARS
PRE-SCHOOL AWARD
PB ISBN: 978-0-00-717765-3 £5.99

Board book ISBN:
978-0-00-714214-9 £4.99

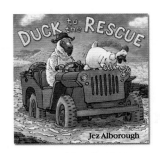

Board book ISBN:
978-0-00-718279-4 £4.99

Board book ISBN:
978-0-00-720927-9 £5.99

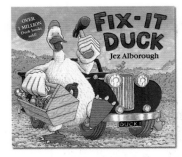

Board book ISBN:
978-0-00-724357-0 £5.99

Jez Alborough was born and grew up in Kingston upon Thames. He graduated from art school in Norwich with a BA Honours degree in Graphic Design. Since then, he has created more than thirty children's picture books. Jez's funny stories about Duck have sold more than one and half million copies worldwide, firmly establishing him as one of today's most talented author/illustrators. Jez lives with his wife in London.

To find out more about Duck visit: JezAlborough.com

THIS BLOOMSBURY BOOK

BELONGS TO

....

For Elsie & Emile – M.R.

For Emily – A.R.

Bloomsbury Publishing, London, Berlin and New York

First published in Great Britain in September 2009 by Bloomsbury Publishing Plc
36 Soho Square, London, W1D 3QY

This paperback edition first published in July 2010

Text copyright © Michael Rosen 2009
Illustrations copyright © Adrian Reynolds 2009
The moral rights of the author and illustrator have been asserted

Audio CD produced by Jeff Capel. Recorded and mixed at the Soundhouse Studios by Paul Deeley
Read by Michael Rosen

Copyright in the recording Ⓒ and Ⓟ Bloomsbury Publishing 2009

A CIP catalogue record of this book is available from the British Library

ISBN 978 0 7475 9796 4

Printed in China by Printplus Limited., Shenzhen, Guangdong

3 5 7 9 10 8 6 4 2

All papers used by Bloomsbury Publishing are natural, recyclable products
made from wood grown in well-managed forests. The manufacturing processes
conform to the environmental regulations of the country of origin

www.bloomsbury.com/childrens

Bear Flies High

Michael Rosen

Illustrated by Adrian Reynolds

BLOOMSBURY

LONDON BERLIN NEW YORK

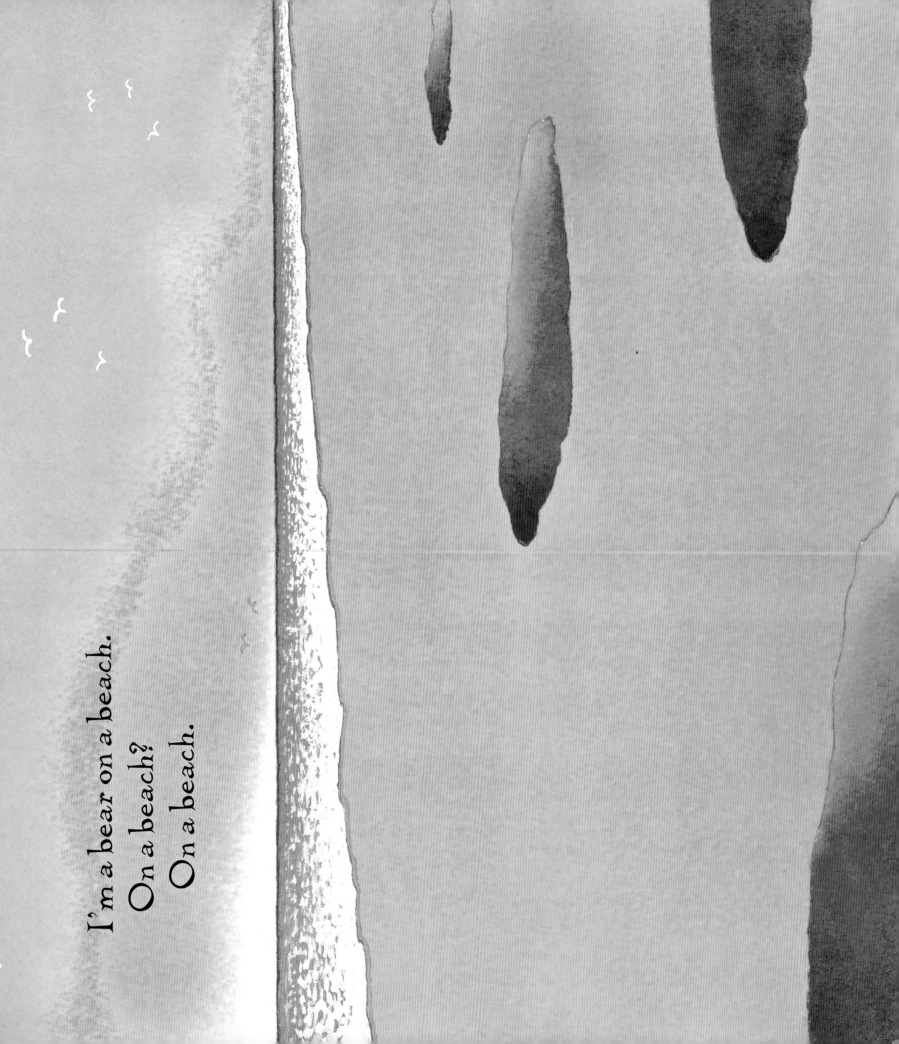

I'm a bear on a beach. On a beach? On a beach.

And I sing by the sea all day.
Doo bee doo
Doo bee doo
Doo bee doodily doo.

I watch the birds in the sky.
In the sky?
In the sky.

And they fly above me up high.
Swoopy swoop
Swoopy swoop
Swoopy swoop
Swoopy swoopity swoop.

I wish I could fly up high.
Up high?
Up high!

I wish I could fly up high one day.

Swoopy swoop

Swoopy swoop

Swoopy swoop

Swoopy swoopity swoop.

'If you want to fly, Mr Bear, follow us.'
'Follow you?'
'Follow us.
Follow us to a place far away.'

Follow, follow

Follow, follow

Follow follity follow.

We're waiting at the gate.
At the gate?
At the gate.

We're waiting at the gate to get in.
Don't push!
Don't push!
Don't pushity push!

Cups and saucers whirling round.
Whirling round?
Whirling round.

Cups and saucers whirling round all day.
Whirly whirl
Whirly whirl
Whirly whirlity whirl.

Haunted house whooping loud.
Whooping loud?
Whooping loud.

Haunted house whooping loud all day.
Hoo woo
Hoo woo
Hoo woopity woo!

Big flipper flying high.
Flying high?
Flying high.

Big flipper flying high in the sky.
Whooshy whoosh
Whooshy whoosh
Whooshy whooshity whoosh.

'You can fly up there, Mr Bear.'
'Up there?'
'Up there.
You can fly up there, if you dare.'

Scary scare

Scary scare

Scary scarety scare.

I'm a bear who can fly!
You can fly?
I can fly.

I can fly in the sky like a bird up high.
Swoopy swoop
Swoopy swoop
Swoopy swoopity swoop.

Then it's back down the road.
Down the road?
Down the road.

Back down the road to get home.
Follow follow
Follow follow
Follow follity follow.

We watch the birds in the sky.
In the sky?
In the sky.
We watch the birds in the sky up high.

Swoopy swoopity swooooooo

And we sing by the sea all day.
Doo bee doo
Doo bee doo

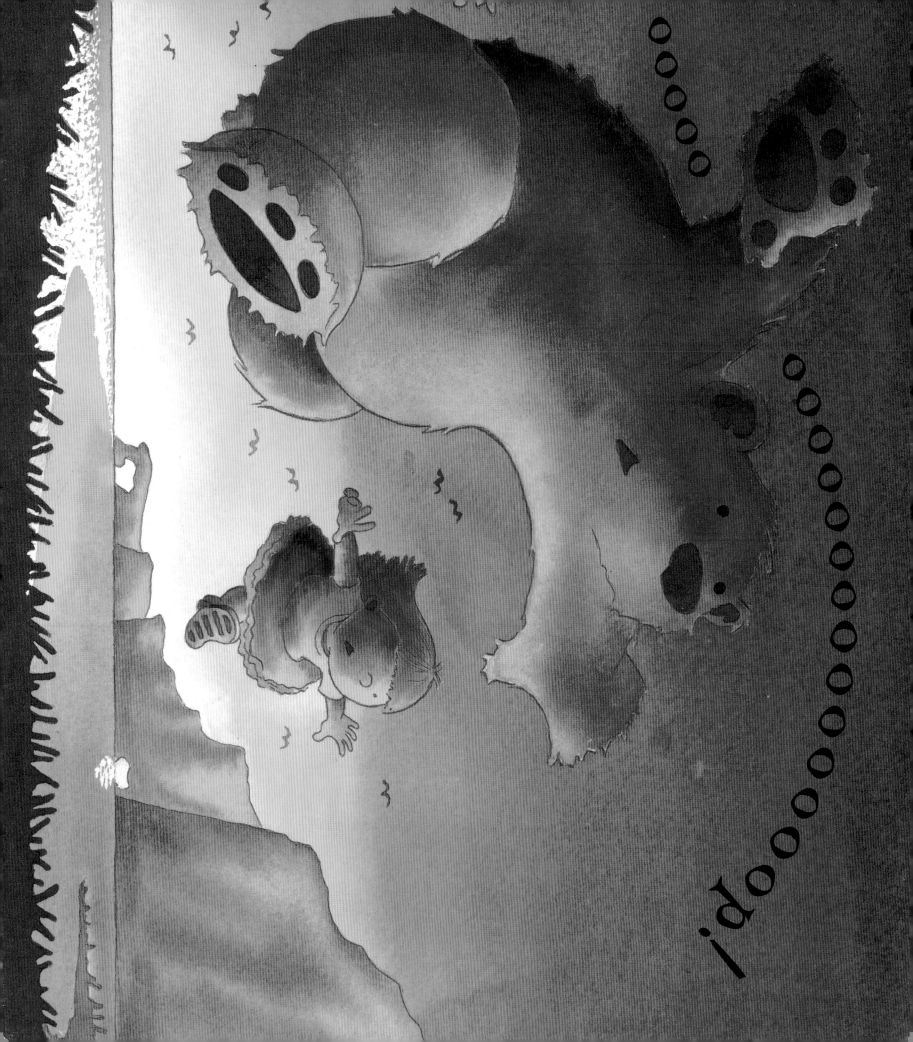

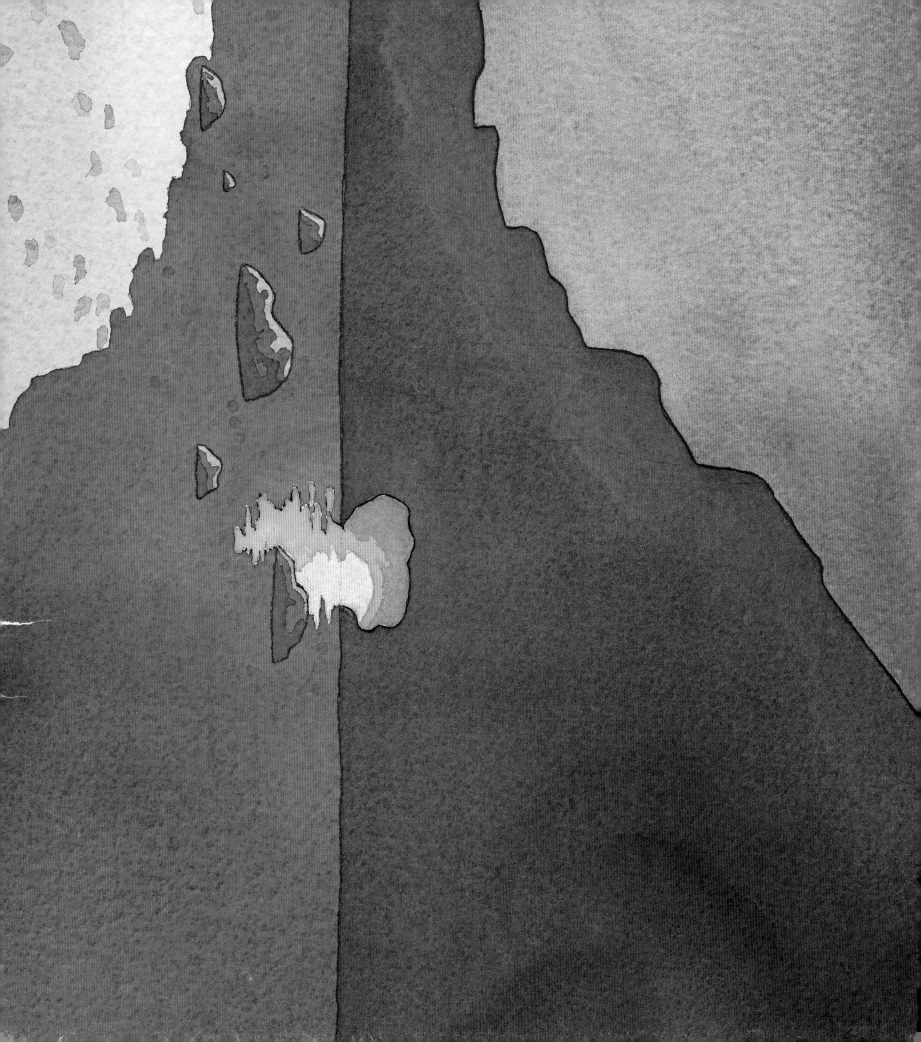

More entertaining tales from Michael Rosen…

The Bear in the Cave
by Michael Rosen & illustrated by Adrian Reynolds

'A long-awaited near-sequel to the bestselling,
much-chanted *We're Going on a Bear Hunt*'
Guardian

Howler
by Michael Rosen & illustrated by Neal Layton

'Rosen's child's-eye humour makes this a superb
means of empathising with a child
who's a bit miffed about a new arrival'
Observer

Rover
by Michael Rosen & illustrated by Neal Layton

'A delight to behold'
Scotsman